Firefighters Fight Fires

Penelope Santos

Rosen REAL READERS

Rosen Classroom™
New York

This is a firefighter.

His job is to put out fires.

Firefighters work with other firefighters. They work at a fire station.

A house is on fire.
Someone calls the fire station.
They need the firefighters
to come quickly!

The firefighters put on fire suits. These will protect them from the fire.

The firefighters get in a fire truck.
They race to the house.

Fire spreads
through the house.
Smoke and fire come out
of the windows.

A firefighter climbs a ladder.
He will see if anyone
is in the house.

Another firefighter gets a hose.
He connects it to a hydrant.
The hydrant shoots water
through the hose.

The firefighters point the hose
at the fire.
They spray water with the hose.

Water puts out fires.

The firefighter sprays the fire.

The fire is put out.

Words to Know

fire

firefighter

hydrant

ladder